For my lovely mum,
Jean MacCarthy,
who is my constant source
of inspiration.

Text and illustrations copyright © Patricia MacCarthy 2013
First published in Great Britain and in the USA in 2013 by
Frances Lincoln Children's Books, 3 Torriano Mews,
Torriano Avenue, London NW5 2RZ
www.franceslincoln.com

A catalogue record for this book is available from the British Library.

ISBN 978-1-84780-283-5

Illustrated with watercolour and coloured pencils

Set in Felt Tip and Floridian Script

Printed in Dongguan, Guangdong, China by Toppan Leefung
9 8 7 6 5 4 3 2 1

Moon Forest

Patricia MacCarthy

F
FRANCES LINCOLN
CHILDREN'S BOOKS

The great white
eye of the
moon
looks into the
forest.

What can it see?

A flitter of bats.

A coil of ferns.

A twist of briars.

A dusting of moths.

A red fox running through a blue forest...

An owl gliding between shadows.

A warm breeze ruffling fur; a hunter's nose sniffing the sweet night air, something stirring, a rat scuttling.

Watching. Listening.

An owl fading into darkness, clutching its prey.

The fox focused, alert and ready to pounce.

Look, see how the Moon Forest jumps
when the fox pounces, and the pheasant
explodes from its hide-out!

Alarmed, a hedgehog
grabs and runs away
with its crunchy beetle snack.

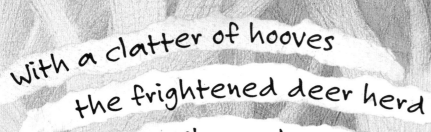

With a clatter of hooves
the frightened deer herd
stampedes deep into the forest.

A hare stands bolt upright
in the Moon's glare, and trembles with fright.

The Moon's eye swivels to watch as...

with pricked ears and

twitching nose

a rabbit crouches low.

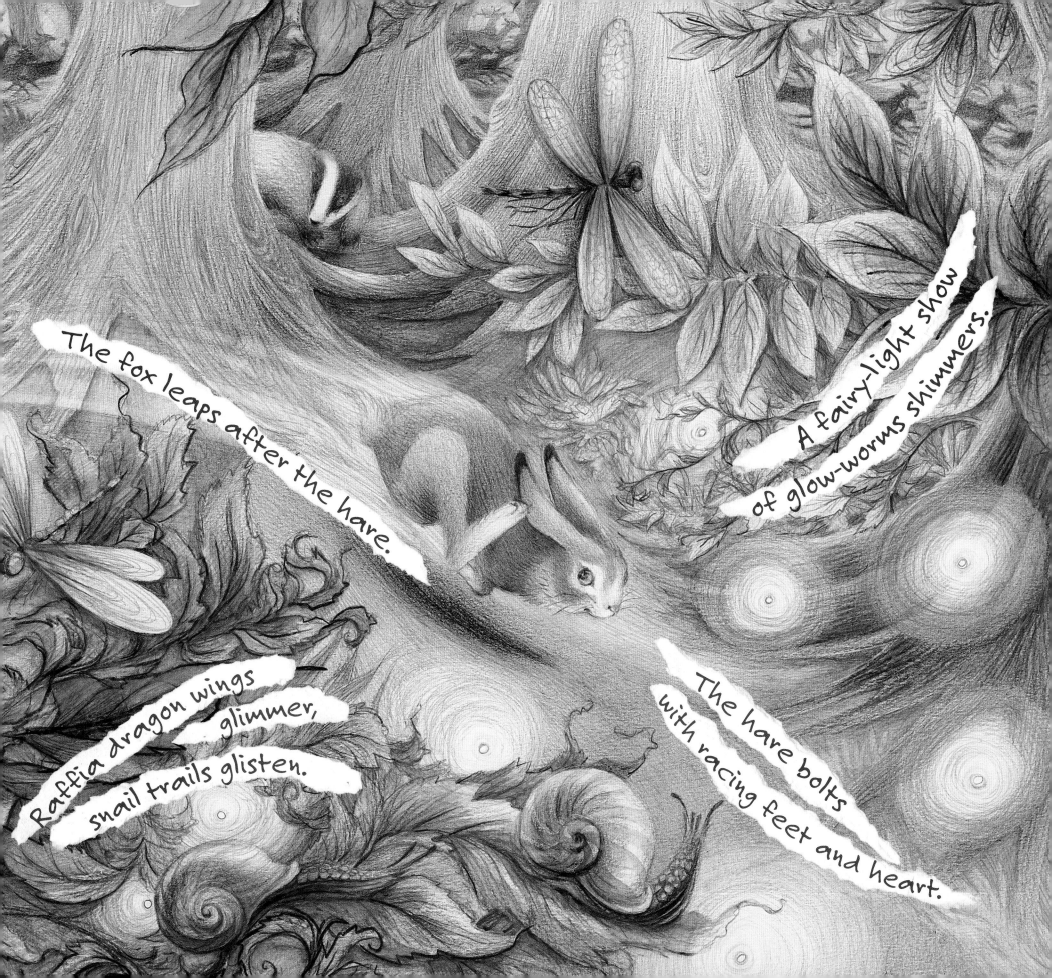

The fox leaps after the hare.

A fairy-light show of glow-worms shimmers.

Raffia dragon wings glimmer, snail trails glisten.

The hare bolts with racing feet and heart.

The searching eye of the Moon
probes the forest.
What does it see?

A slippery fish caught
and devoured by
a sleek and silky otter.

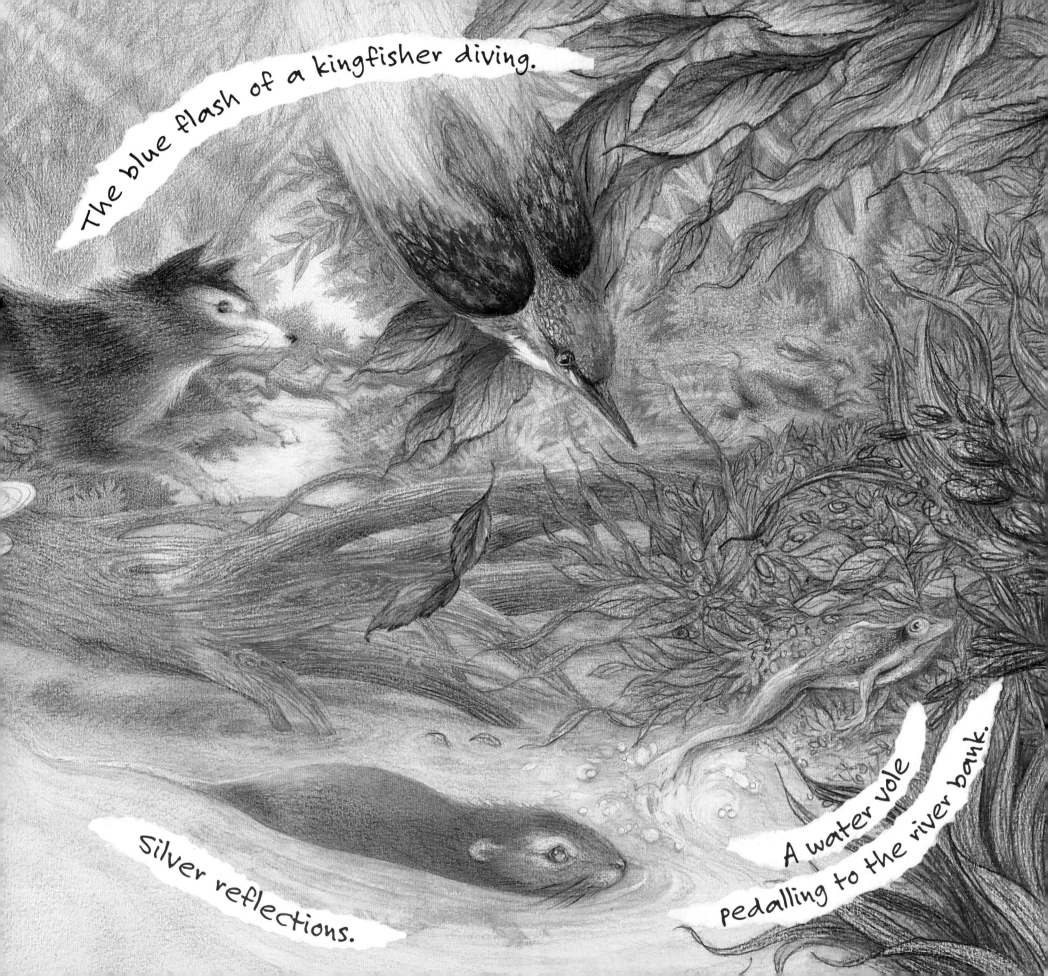

Thudding feet.
Pounding heart.
Earth and whiskers.

A family of badgers comes up from the sett to sniff the sweet night air.

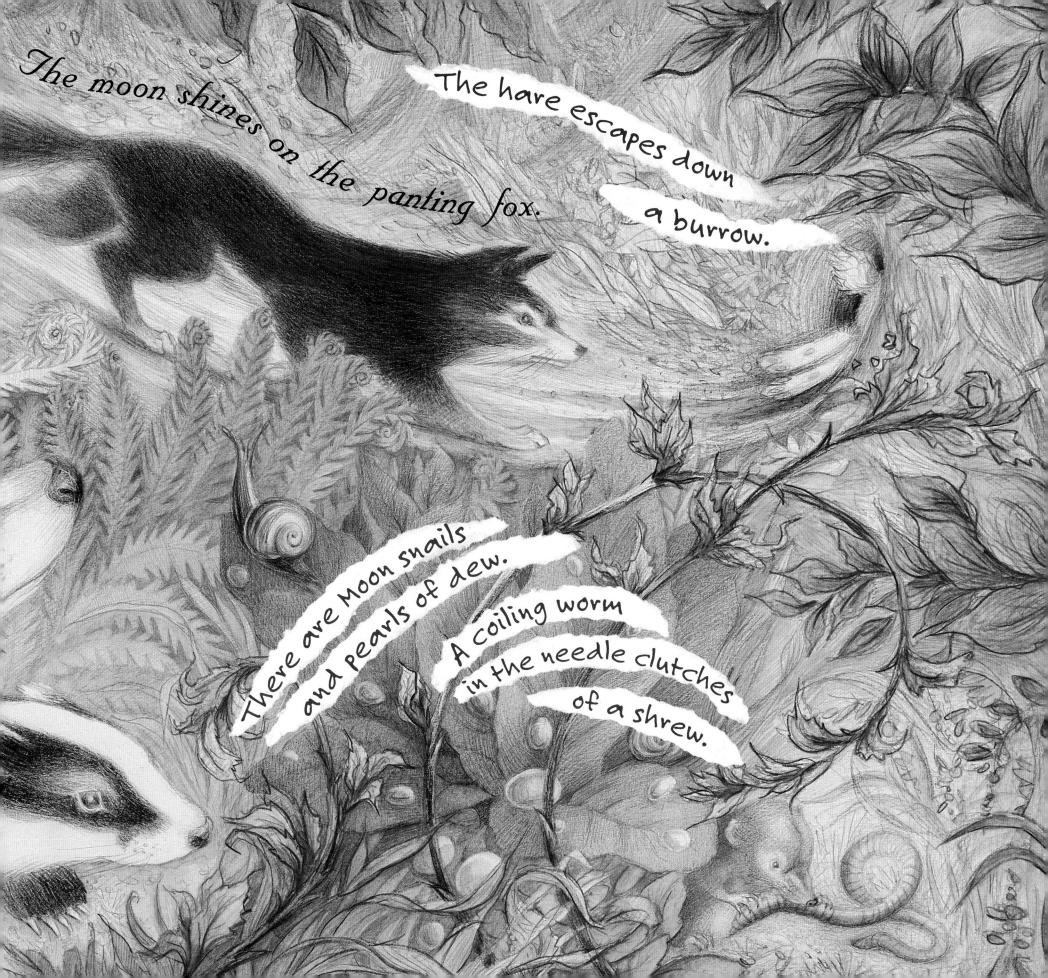

The moon shines on the panting fox.

The hare escapes down a burrow.

There are moon snails and pearls of dew.

A coiling worm in the needle clutches of a shrew.

All around is rustling, fluttering, scratching
and clattering as the Moon Forest
creatures hunt and forage...

All is stirring, the forest is alive.

but the hungry fox must rest.

The creatures of the forest
stare back at the
great white eye of the moon.
And what do they see?

and survival!